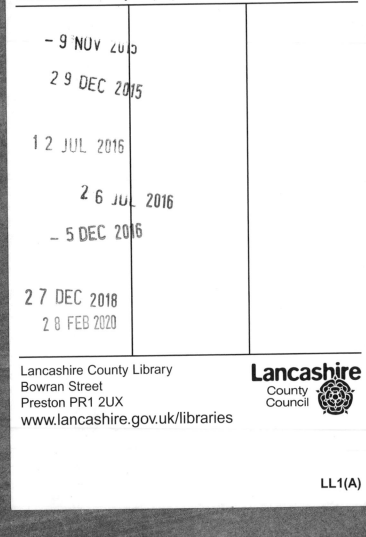

Marc Martin is an award-winning illustrator based in Melbourne,
Australia. Working with a variety of mediums, Marc's work is a
world of dense colour, rich textures and the odd scribble.
More of his artwork can be found at www.marcmartin.com

He received the 2013 Crichton Award for Australia's best new illustrator
for his first picture book, *A Forest*.

A TEMPLAR BOOK

First published in the UK in 2015 by Templar Publishing,
an imprint of The Templar Company Limited,
Deepdene Lodge, Deepdene Avenue, Dorking, Surrey, RH5 4AT, UK
www.templarco.co.uk

First published by Penguin Group (Australia), 2014

First edition

ISBN 978-1-78370-196-4

Cover and internal design by Marc Martin and Bruno Herfst

Printed in China

Max

by Marc Martin

templar publishing

This is Max.

Max lives by the sea.
You might have seen Max before.

He's a little bit cheeky,
and a little bit mischievous.

But mostly, he's a very nice seagull.

There are two things Max likes.

He likes fish.

And he likes chips.

Oh, and he also
likes Bob!

Max and Bob are
very old friends.

Max visits Bob
every day.

He keeps him company,
and greets the customers
as they come in.

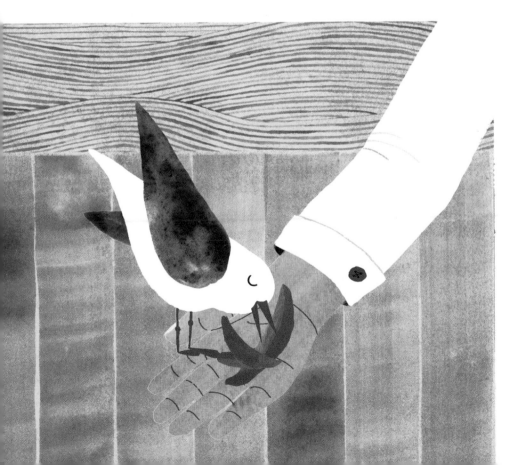

If Max behaves himself, Bob
gives him a few chips.

In the evenings, Max and Bob
go fishing together.

And when the sun goes down,
Bob says, "See you tomorrow, Max!"

But one summer, the shop was very quiet,
and there were fewer customers to greet.

Bob seemed sad.
Even a freshly caught fish couldn't cheer him up.

The next time Max came to visit,
Bob was gone.

So Max waited.

He waited a day.

He waited a week.

He waited a very,
very long time.

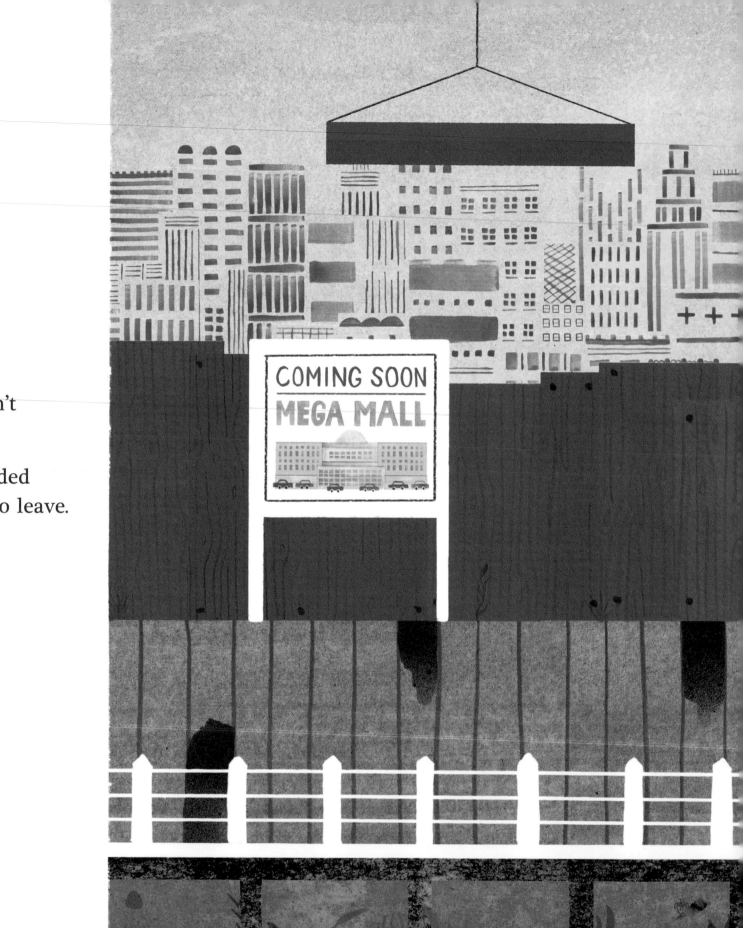

But Bob didn't
come back.

So Max decided
it was time to leave.

He flew high
into the sky.

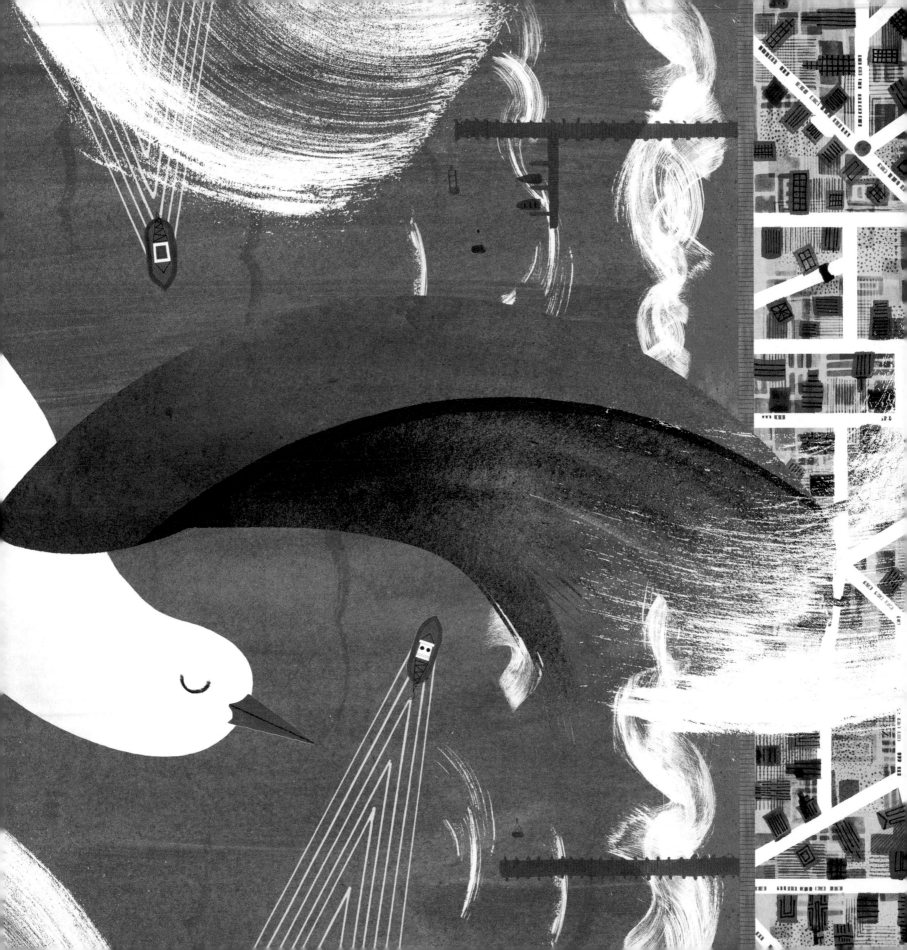

As he flew, Max saw many things,

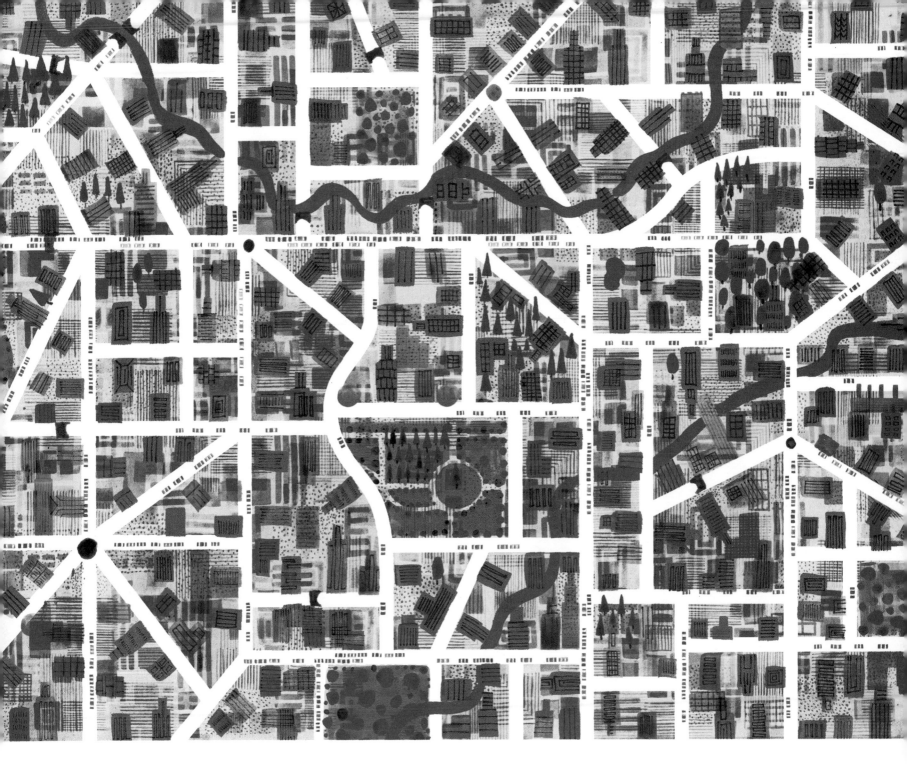

but where was Bob?

Then Max smelt something familiar...

So he followed the smell –

over the trees,

around the city,

and above the tall
buildings.

Until he came to a shop.

A chip shop.

It was Bob's shop!

It was a brand new shop,
but there was still a place
for Max to sit.

"Max!" said Bob.
"How did you find me?
I thought I'd never see
you again! I missed you."

Now Max visits Bob
in the city every day.

You might see him there
on his best behaviour.
He greets the customers
and waits patiently
for a chip.

And in the evenings,
Bob closes the shop,

BOB & MAX'S

Closed

they head to the ocean…